Lleonard
The Llama
That LIED

by
Susan Cameron

illustrated by
Mark A. Hicks

Paulist Press
New York/Mahwah, N.J.

Book design by Mark A. Hicks

Library of Congress Cataloging in Publication Data

Cameron, Susan, 1960–
    Lleonard the Llama that lied / by Susan Cameron : illustrated by Mark Hicks.
      p.   cm.
    Summary: A young llama that enjoys lying and playing tricks on other animals learns a lesson when he becomes invisible after eating a magical flower.
    ISBN 0-8091-6636-4 (alk. paper)
    [1. Llamas—Fiction. 2. Honesty—Fiction. 3. Behavior—Fiction. 4. Stories in rhyme.] I. Hicks, Mark A., ill. II. Title.
    PZ8.3.C136L1 1997
    [E]—dc20   96-38539
                                            CIP
                                            AC

Published by Paulist Press
997 Macarthur Boulevard
Mahwah, New Jersey 07430

Printed and bound in the United States of America

For My Parents:
Harold and Peg MacDonald

Just over the border—
In the hills of Bofrad—
Lived a llama named Lleonard
Who loved to be bad.

He scared Sammy Squirrel,
And threw rocks at Fox Frye,
But his most favorite badness
Was—Lleonard loved *lies*.

"Hey, Bernie—" said Lleonard—
"Honey drips from those trees!"
When the bear reached inside—
He got stung by mad bees!

"There are berries galore
Down the prickly path—"
And when Chippy got stuck—
Then young Lleonard would laugh.

And the smallest of birds
And the biggest of beasts
Grew so mad at young Lleonard—
"He lies and he cheats—"

"Beware of that Llama—"
And their heads shook again.
Soon Lleonard the Llama
Found himself with no friends.

Then one day young Lleonard—
While a-sniffing around—
Found a lone bright red flower
Sprung up from the ground.

"How delicious!" he thought—
"Set apart from the bunch."
Then Lleonard the Llama
Settled down to have lunch.

No sooner had Lleonard
Taken one sweet red bite
When he felt his whole body
Begin to get tight.

"I'm shrinking!" cried Lleonard—
"Someone help—This is weird!"
And he shrunk and he shrunk
And then—poof!—disappeared.

So Lleonard cried "Help!"
Through the hills and the trees—
But the others below
Could hear only the breeze.

And he ran through the hills
And he shouted and sighed
And finally at sunset—
Lleonard broke down and cried.

And—lo—from beneath him—
In the midst of his fret
Came a voice—"Cut it out there—
I'm getting all wet!"

And a grumbly toad
Crawled on up Lleonard's nose—
"Enough of this noise—
And enough of these woes!"

"Bly's the name," said the toad.
"You're not looking so well.
That's a magical flower—
Seems you're under a spell."

"A spell?!" Lleonard wailed—
"All I wanted was lunch!
But—why can only *you* see me?"
Said Bly—"I've a hunch…"

"I can see in the dark—
I can see underground—
I see things no one else can—
Pal—I've been around."

"I've seen one magic flower
Teach all kinds of weird things—
Sometimes birds learn to bark—
Even toads start to sing."

"You've got something to learn—
What?—I haven't a clue.
But you sure can't ask others.
So—the answer's in you."

"You're kidding!" cried Lleonard—
"No thank you, I'll pass.
I'd like to show up here,
Not to sign up for class."

"Have it your way," Bly shrugged—
And before Lleonard could blink—
Bly left him—unseen
And unheard of—to think.

But though no one could see
Or hear *him* anymore—
Lleonard started to see
What he hadn't before.

He watched Mrs. Rabbit
Teach her young how to run—
How to hop through the fields—
How to bask in the sun.

He hopped alongside them,
And he rolled in the hay
With the ponies whose mother
Would teach them to play.

"How I miss my mother
And the friends I've not had.
How I wish—oh, I do wish—
I hadn't been bad!"

And suddenly, near him—
As he spoke these sad words—
Lleonard saw Sammy Squirrel
Tell a lie to Bo Bird.

"Hey, Bo—are you hungry?
There's some corn on the ground."
And Bo searched and she searched—
But there was none to be found.

And Lleonard looked up,
And he heard hungry cries,
And he saw Bo's new babies,
And the hope in Bo's eyes.

And something happened to Lleonard
As he witnessed the scene—
What Sammy called fun
Lleonard saw was just *mean*!

"Cut that out!" Lleonard yelled—
"Now look what you've done—
It's no fun to lie—
You're just hurting someone!"

And the message—though soundless—
Still pierced like a dart
Through the squirrel's left ear—
And went straight to his heart.

And so Lleonard had found—
Though Non-Llama in word
And Non-Lama in sight—
A new way to be heard—

When he spoke from his heart,
The message always came through—
Ringing deep inside all
In a voice loud and true.

And lastly young Lleonard—
As he walked on alone—
Found himself near Old Hump Nook
And headed toward home.

As he entered his house
And saw Mother alone
Lleonard wished for her hug
And was glad he was home.

To be seen, to be loved—
What a simple, great joy.
"Mother, it's Lleonard—
And I've been a bad boy."

"But I took a long trip
With a magical start,
Now I know what "truth" is—
It's what lives in our heart."

"And right now—of all truths—
One's most-most-mostly true—
I'm the luckiest Llama—
With a mother like you!"

And with these words young Lleonard
Just started to grow
From the depths of his heart
To his last Llama toe—

And he grew and he grew
And he grew to full size.
He was no longer shrunk
From his badness and lies.

And now Lleonard the Llama
spends his time playing right—
And he speaks in heard words
And he stands in full sight—

And he tells all the young ones
Of beast and of bird,
"Tell the truth—just remember—
It's the way to be heard!"